PuPPy

This book is for LES . . . with love and kisses.

Library of Congress catalog card number: 63-7809

The publishers are grateful to the following for permission to reprint copyrighted material: Thomas Y. Crowell Company, New York, for "Found, the Little Lost Dog," by Val Teal, from *Read Me More Stories,* compiled by the Child Study Association of America, © Copyright, 1951, by Thomas Y. Crowell Company; Jean F. Merrill for "A Dog for Davy," © Copyright, 1953, by *Story-A-Day;* Irma Simonton Black for "Spoodles: The Puppy Who Learned," © Copyright, 1948, by Irma Simonton Black.

Dog Tales

SELECTED AND WITH VERSES BY
NITA JONAS
PICTURES BY
DALE MAXEY

RANDOM HOUSE   NEW YORK

Your puppy
will always
be your friend
For it's
you he's
thinking of,
So always
give him a great big hug
And lots and lots of love.

You can give your pup a bath
when he's four months old,
But keep him warm, wrapped
in a towel   So puppy won't
catch
cold.

Found, the Little Lost Dog
by Val Teal

Mother took John and Peter downtown to buy new shoes. They parked their car and got out. A little gray dog was sitting on the sidewalk. He sniffed at John and Peter and whined. They patted his head. He jumped up and tried to lick their faces.

"He likes us," Peter said. "Can't we keep him for our dog?"

"No," Mother said. "He's lost. The people who lost him will be looking for him."

When they came back from buying the shoes, the little gray dog was still there. They patted his head.

"Poor little lost dog," they said.

The little lost dog wagged his tail.

"Can't we keep him for our dog?" John said.

"No," Mother said. "He isn't our dog."

Mother opened the car door. John got in. Peter got in. And then, when nobody was looking, the little lost dog got in. He snuggled down on the floor of the back seat.

When they got home Mother got out of the car. John got out. Peter got out. He left the car door open. The little lost dog got out.

"Look!" Peter said. "It's the little lost dog! He followed us home."

The little gray dog shivered.

"Can't he come in and get warm?" John asked.

"Yes," Mother said. "Poor little lost dog."

They found an old rug and put it in the back hall. The little lost dog lay down on it. They found an old blanket and covered him up. The little lost dog went to sleep.

"We found a little lost dog," Peter said.

"He needs a bath," Father said.

They gave the little gray dog a bath. They washed him with soap. They rubbed him with a towel. He stood on the floor and shook himself.

He wasn't a little gray dog! He was a little white dog! With pink linings in his ears. And a little black nose with pink edges. And a long pink tongue. And beautiful big brown eyes.

They fed him and gave him a saucer of milk.

"Can't we keep him?" Peter asked.

"He isn't our dog," Father said. "We must try to find his owners." They looked in the evening paper. Nobody had advertised for a little lost white dog.

"Can we keep him now?" John asked.

"No," Father said. "We must try to find his owners." They took him to a place where all the lost dogs are. They left him there to see if his owners would come and get him. They left him there three days.

After three days they went back. There was the little lost dog. Nobody had come to get him. He was sitting in the corner of a pen. He looked very sad. When he saw them he jumped up and ran to meet them. He licked their hands.

"Poor little lost dog," Peter said.

"He isn't lost any more," Father said.

"Can we keep him?" John and Peter shouted.

"Yes," Father said. "Now he is our dog."

They took the little lost dog home. He snuggled on the rug in the back hall. They covered him up with the blanket. He went to sleep. He looked very happy. He didn't look lost.

"Look," Peter said. "He's found." So they named the little lost dog Found. And to this very day Found is living with John and Peter and sleeping on the rug in the back hall.

Take a bowl
of water
    And give
some to
    your pup,
For puppies
    do get thirsty
And love to
    lap it up!

On Wednesday, Davy walked down to the firehouse to talk with the firemen. The firemen had a sleek white dog with black spots.

"What kind of dog is that?" Davy asked.

"That's a coach hound," said the fireman. "A firehouse doesn't look right unless it has a coach hound sitting in front of it."

Davy didn't have a firehouse. But he thought a spotted coach hound would look nice sitting in front of *his* house.

When his father came home from work, Davy ran to meet him.

"Daddy, I've decided to have a coach hound," he said.

"All right," said his father, "if that's what you want."

The next day was Thursday. Only two days till Davy's birthday.

Davy saw a man hanging up a circus poster on the fence across the street. On the poster was a pert little white dog riding a tricycle.

"What kind of dog is that?" Davy asked the man.

"That's a terrier," said the poster hanger. "Terriers are very good circus dogs because they are very clever at learning tricks."

Davy didn't have a circus. But he thought it would be nice to have a little dog that did tricks.

He told his father that night, "A terrier is the kind of dog I want."

"That's all right with me," said his father.

The next day was Friday, the day before Davy's birthday. Davy went to the beach to sail his boat. There he saw two little girls playing with a plump, wiggly little dog with long curly hair.

"What kind of dog is that?" asked Davy.

"It's a spaniel," said the little girls. "Spaniels are very good swimmers."

Davy couldn't swim but he thought it would be nice to have a dog who could.

That night, he told his father, "I think I'll have a spaniel."

Daddy smiled. "All right," he said. "We'll go shopping for your dog tomorrow."

It was Saturday at last, Davy's birthday. Daddy took him to the dog store. There were collies and there were setters. There were coach hounds and terriers and spaniels.

Which kind did Davy want most? When he saw all the dogs together, he didn't know. Each kind was nicest in its own way. He couldn't decide which he wanted most. Then suddenly Davy saw, way back in a corner of the dog store, a different kind of dog. It was a little black dog with a brown spot on its chest and a white tip on its tail. It was a long-legged, short-haired dog with one ear that stood up and one that flopped down. He was a funny, friendly little dog, and his white-tipped tail waved gaily when he saw Davy.

"What kind of dog is that?" Davy asked the man who ran the dog shop.

"That's no particular kind at all," said the man. "It's a mixture of all kinds. It's a bit of spaniel and a bit of terrier. A bit of collie and a bit of coach hound, with a bit of setter thrown in for good measure. In fact," said the man, "it's just a dog."

Davy looked at the little black dog. Then he looked at his father.

"*That's* the dog I want," he said,
"*most of all.*"

When a puppy wags his tail
It means he's feeling glad.

But when his tail is quiet . . .
The puppy dog is sad.

Puppy dogs get tired
   And like to take a nap.
Their favorite place for sleeping
   Is plop! Right on your lap!

SPOODLES, the Puppy Who Learned

by Irma Simonton Black

Once there was a funny little dog.
He wasn't quite a spaniel—
a spaniel looks like this:

He wasn't quite a poodle—a poodle
looks like this:

He looked like both of them at once,
so he was called Spoodles.

Of all the dogs in town—big dogs, little dogs, long dogs, short dogs, fat dogs, thin dogs—Spoodles was the only Spoodle.

All the dogs liked Spoodles, but his best friend was Rowdy, who lived next door.

Spoodles was Connie's dog, and they played together a lot. The game they liked the best was chase-the-ball. Connie rolled the red ball and Spoodles raced after it and brought it back in his mouth.

Spoodles' family loved him very much.

Mother said, "What a good dog Spoodles is! He is better than a spaniel."

Father said, "He is better than a poodle."

Connie said, "He is as good as a spoodle, and that is very, very good." But once Spoodles' family went away for the day. They couldn't take Spoodles with them, so they left him all alone in the house. Connie wasn't there to play ball with him. He couldn't get out to play with Rowdy.

Spoodles was LONELY! He put back his head and made his mouth in a round shape and

HOWLED!

After he howled, he felt better, because he couldn't feel worse. If he couldn't play with Rowdy, he would have to find something else to do. He trotted sadly from one room to another. There was no one in the living room. There was no one in the dining room. There was no one in the kitchen. Sadly he climbed the stairs. Connie's room was empty. There was no one in the bathroom. But under Father's bed in the big front bedroom, Spoodles saw something hiding.

It was something furry hiding under the bed, waiting to pounce on him when he wasn't looking. Spoodles growled at it. Then he barked at it. Then he circled around it carefully, because it looked fierce. When he was behind it, suddenly he jumped on it, caught it by the throat, and shook it. It was quite a battle, but when it was over, Spoodles lay on the rug, dreamily chewing on Father's slipper.

After a while Spoodles began to get lonely again, so he went downstairs to look for something else to do. In the kitchen he found a tomato. It was round and red and roly, like a ball. Spoodles rolled it down the cellar stairs to see if it would bounce. It didn't. Spoodles needed another ball, so he went back to the vegetable bin. He took a second tomato carefully in his teeth and trotted upstairs with it. He went past Mother's and Father's room, past the bathroom, straight into Connie's room, and he jumped up on Connie's bed.

He pushed the tomato with his nose and squeezed it between his teeth. That was the way he played with his ball. The tomato split open. He tried to play with it some more, but it was a very splashy

.ball, so he left it right in the middle of Connie's bed.

When he got back to the kitchen he smelled something good. The smell came from the garbage pail. First he found a piece of bread. That wasn't the good smell.

Then he found some orange skins.

That wasn't the good smell.

Then he found a pile of coffee grounds.

That wasn't the good smell.

He dug deeper in the garbage and out came some eggshells.

That wasn't the good smell.

At the very bottom Spoodles found a knobby soupbone.

That was the good smell!

When Spoodles had chewed the soupbone all he wanted, he looked for a place to bury it. The floor was too hard. He tried the sofa in the living room. That was better!

When the bone was buried, Spoodles felt sleepy, so he curled up and went to sleep. He wasn't lonesome any more.

A long time later, Spoodles woke up. He heard a tiny rattle. It was the sound of a key in the lock. His family were home! Spoodles ran to meet them, wagging his short tail so fast that it looked like several tails. Spoodles' family were glad to see him too, until . . . Connie turned on the kitchen light.

"What a mess!" said Father as he started down the cellar to look at the furnace.

Spoodles could tell by their voices that something was wrong. He wondered if he was wrong.

"Doggone that doggone slippery tomato! Nearly broke my doggone neck!" shouted Father as he got to the bottom of the stairs. Spoodles began to think for sure that he was wrong.

Even Connie didn't seem to understand about the ball game Spoodles had played with the tomato on her nice clean white bedspread.

"Look at this!" said Father, when he saw his slipper. "All chewed up. Insides pulled out. Heel gone."

By this time Spoodles was very, very sad. He wondered if his family would ever love him again.

But the worst of all was when they saw the living room.

Mother said, "He is worse than a spaniel."

Father said, "He is worse than a poodle."

Connie said, "He is as bad as a spoodle, and right now that is very, very bad."

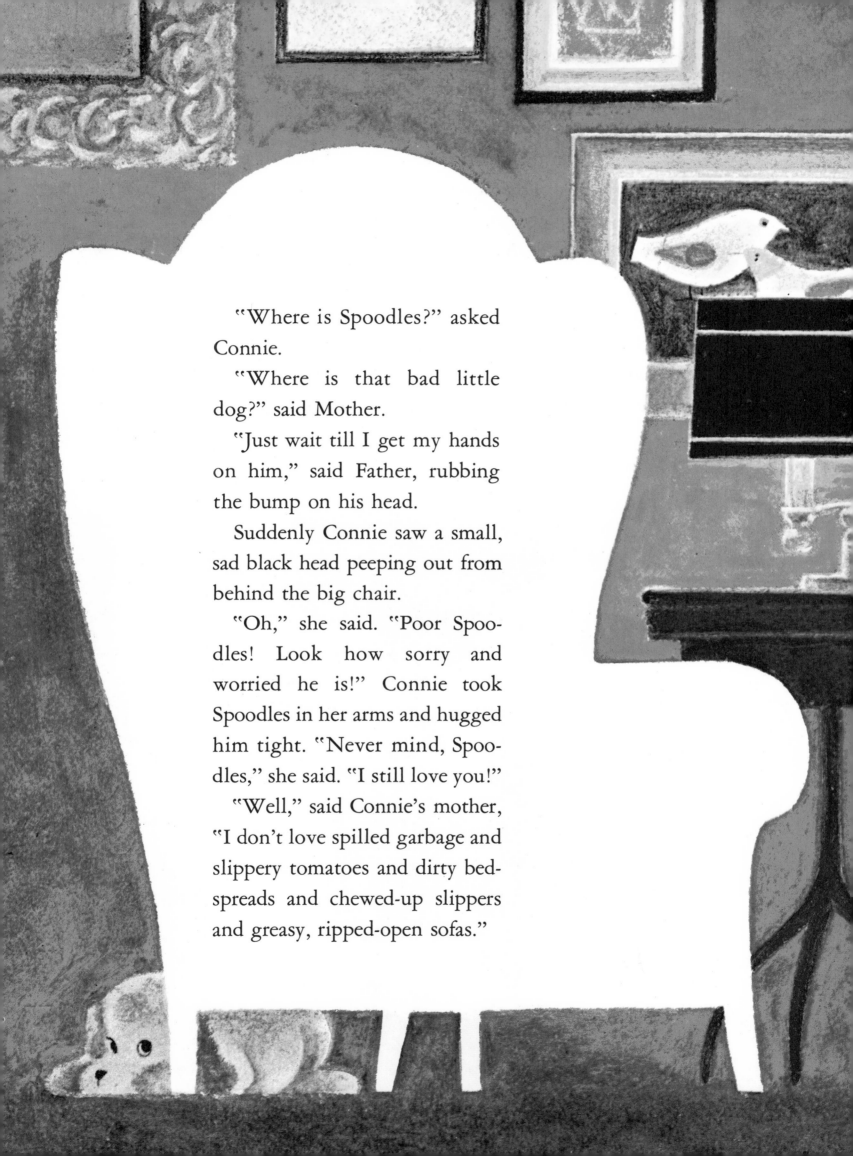

"Where is Spoodles?" asked Connie.

"Where is that bad little dog?" said Mother.

"Just wait till I get my hands on him," said Father, rubbing the bump on his head.

Suddenly Connie saw a small, sad black head peeping out from behind the big chair.

"Oh," she said. "Poor Spoodles! Look how sorry and worried he is!" Connie took Spoodles in her arms and hugged him tight. "Never mind, Spoodles," she said. "I still love you!"

"Well," said Connie's mother, "I don't love spilled garbage and slippery tomatoes and dirty bedspreads and chewed-up slippers and greasy, ripped-open sofas."

"Neither do I," said Connie's father, "but it was partly our fault too. We shouldn't have left so young a dog alone in the house all day. If we tell him never to do it again, I think he will understand."

"Spoodles, we won't ever leave you for so long," they said, "but you must never, never, never spill the garbage. You must never squash tomatoes on a bed. And never leave one on the cellar stairs. Or ever chew up slippers or bury another bone in the sofa. Not ever, ever, ever again."

Spoodles listened very carefully when they talked to him. He tilted his head to one side to hear better. Spoodles' eyes shone happily and the pink tip of his tongue hung out of his mouth. Then he kissed Connie right on the tip of her nose because she and her family still loved him.